THE SHARK ATTACKS OF 1916

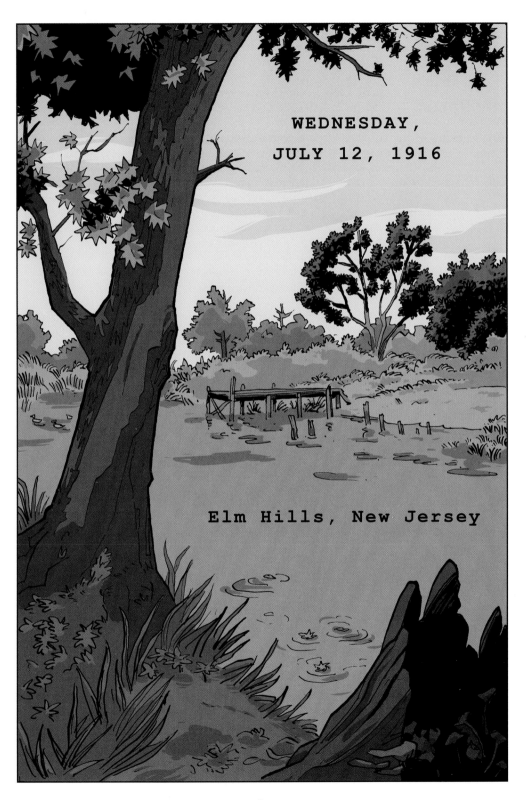

WEDNESDAY,
JULY 12, 1916

Elm Hills, New Jersey

I CAN FEEL IT.

LIKE A CHILL DEEP DOWN IN MY BONES.

SOMEONE—

—OR SOMETHING—

—IS WATCHING ME.

2

AND THEN I SEE IT.

COULD IT REALLY BE . . .

A SHARK?

THAT'S IMPOSSIBLE!

ELM HILLS IS MILES AND MILES FROM THE OCEAN.

A SHARK COULDN'T FIND ITS WAY INTO THIS LITTLE CREEK.

BUT—

IT'S COMING TOWARD ME.

BLACK EYES WATCHING ME.

KILLER EYES.

SPLASH!

I SWIM WITH ALL MY MIGHT.

IT'S RIGHT BEHIND ME!

JAWS WIDE—

—WHITE DAGGER TEETH GLEAMING—

—MOUTH BLOODRED.

I SURVIVED

THE SHARK ATTACKS OF 1916

BASED ON THE NOVEL IN THE *NEW YORK TIMES*
BESTSELLING SERIES BY LAUREN TARSHIS

ADAPTED BY GEORGIA BALL
WITH ART BY HAUS STUDIO
PENCILS BY GERVASIO
INKS BY JOK AND CARLOS AÓN
COLORS BY LARA LEE
ART ASSISTANCE BY DARIO BRABO
LOGO AND FONTS BY CARLOS AÓN

graphix
AN IMPRINT OF
■SCHOLASTIC

THE MONDAY MORNING BREAKFAST RUSH IS FINALLY OVER.

ELM HILLS DINER

MY FEET ACHE AND I'M COVERED IN SYRUP, BUT I DON'T MIND.

UNCLE JERRY IS PAYING ME A SMALL FORTUNE TO HELP OUT THIS SUMMER.

FIFTEEN CENTS A DAY!

HEY, CHET, DID YOU HEAR?

YOU WON'T BELIEVE IT!

LET ME TELL HIM.

IT WAS A SHARK!

HAPPENED RIGHT IN BEACH HAVEN.

IT WAS HUGE!

THERE WAS BLOOD EVERYWHERE!

SID, DEWEY, AND MONTY NEVER TALKED TO ME AT SCHOOL.

BUT THEY'VE BEEN COMING TO THE DINER EVERY MORNING ON THE WAY TO THEIR OWN SUMMER JOBS.

YOU FELLAS AREN'T TRYING TO FOOL ME, ARE YOU?

I HEARD ABOUT THAT FROG YOU PUT IN MINNIE MARSTON'S LUNCH PAIL.

WE'RE NOT FOOLIN'!

LOOK AT THIS.

"CHARLES VANSANT, TWENTY-FIVE, WAS ATTACKED BY A LARGE SHARK SATURDAY, JULY 1, WHILE SWIMMING IN CHEST-DEEP WATER...

...VACATIONING AT THE LUXURIOUS ENGLESIDE HOTEL...

"THE SHARK BRUTALLY ATTACKED THE YOUNG MAN, WHO STRUGGLED TO SWIM TO SHORE.

"THE GUY WAS A MILLIONAIRE. OWNED A BIG SHIPPING COMPANY.

"ONE DAY, ABOUT TWENTY-FIVE YEARS AGO, THIS GENT WAS OUT ON HIS YACHT WITH HIS RICH FRIENDS JUST OUTSIDE OF NEW YORK CITY.

"THEY SAILED RIGHT THROUGH A BIG SCHOOL OF SHARKS.

"OELRICHS PUT ON HIS BATHING SUIT AND DOVE INTO THE WATER . . .

"PRACTICALLY RIGHT ON TOP OF THOSE SHARKS."

WHY DID HE DO THAT?

TO PROVE THAT THE SHARKS WOULDN'T ATTACK!

"HE MADE A REAL REAL FUSS—SPLASHING, KICKING, AND SHOUTING.

"WOULDN'T YOU KNOW, THE SHARKS SWAM AWAY. THEY WERE SCARED AS RABBITS!"

AFTER THAT, MR. OELRICHS OFFERED A FIVE-HUNDRED-DOLLAR REWARD TO ANYONE WHO COULD COME UP WITH ONE CASE OF A SHARK ATTACKING A HUMAN ON THE NORTHEASTERN COAST.

THAT'S CRAZY!

MAYBE SO, DEWEY . . .

BUT NOBODY EVER COLLECTED THE REWARD.

"THE YEAR WAS 1852.

"IT WAS ONE OF MY FIRST WHALING VOYAGES.

"I WASN'T MUCH OLDER THAN YOU LADS.

"TWO YEARS AT SEA, AND I WAS FINALLY HEADED HOME ACROSS THE PACIFIC.

THE OTHER MEN DIED?

AND THEN I SAW THE FIN.

THE SHARK?

SHHH . . .

"IT CIRCLED ME FOR A LONG WHILE.

"REAL SLOW, LIKE IT WAS TOYING WITH ME.

"LITTLE BY LITTLE, THE BEAST CAME CLOSER, UNTIL I COULD SEE ITS EYES.

"BLACK AS COAL.

"KILLER EYES.

"THE BEAST WENT UNDERWATER . . .

"FOR A SECOND, I THOUGHT IT DECIDED I WASN'T WORTH THE TROUBLE. BUT THEN—

"—SOMETHING BUMPED MY LEG.

"THE SKIN OF A SHARK IS ROUGH, LIKE SANDPAPER.

"IT SCRAPED ME BLOODY!

"AND NOW THERE WAS BLOOD IN THE WATER.

"IT CAME IN FOR THE KILL, WITH JAWS BIG ENOUGH TO SWALLOW ME WHOLE.

"THEN I REMEMBERED THE OLD HARPOON TIP I HAD IN MY POCKET . . ."

BUT SHE PASSED AT LEAST TWENTY YEARS AGO.

POOR OLD GUY. HIS MIND IS LIKE SWISS CHEESE.

YOU MEAN THAT STORY ISN'T TRUE?

I THINK THE CAPTAIN SPINS A MIGHTY FINE TALE.

I STABBED IT WITH A HARPOON TIP!

RIGHT IN ITS KILLER EYE!

NEXT THE CAPTAIN WILL TELL US HE GOT GOBBLED UP BY A WHITE WHALE.

HEH-HEH . . .

YOU'VE LIVED ALL OVER THE PLACE, HAVEN'T YOU, CHET? YOU EVER SEEN THE PACIFIC OCEAN?

SURE.

WHAT'S IT LOOK LIKE?

A LITTLE BLUER THAN THE ATLANTIC. WAVES A LITTLE BIGGER MAYBE.

BUT OTHERWISE JUST LOTS OF WATER AND WAVES.

HOW ABOUT THE MISSISSIPPI RIVER? YOU SEEN THAT TOO?

I WAS ON A STEAMBOAT ONCE THAT GOT STUCK IN THE MUD.

WE HAD TO STAY THERE FOR A WHOLE DAY AND NIGHT.

YOU'RE THE LUCKIEST KID I KNOW!

YEAH?

SURE! TO SEE ALL THOSE PLACES.

I DON'T KNOW. I HATE MOVING AROUND SO MUCH.

HEY, WHY DON'T YOU COME TO THE CREEK WITH US?

WE'RE ALWAYS LOOKING FOR YOU THERE.

IT'S NOT THE PACIFIC OCEAN, BUT IT'S PRETTY NICE.

I BET IT'S BETTER THAN THE PACIFIC!

PAPA WAS ALWAYS CHASING SOME NEW BUSINESS IDEA.

SELLING MOTORCARS IN OREGON . . .

BUILDING BICYCLES IN ST. LOUIS . . .

OR TAKING FAMILY PORTRAITS IN PHILADELPHIA.

POOF

I ALWAYS TRIED TO MAKE FRIENDS, BUT JUST WHEN WE WERE STARTING TO GET COMFORTABLE . . .

BUSINESS WOULD GO BAD OR PAPA WOULD GET SOME OTHER IDEA.

I WAS SUPPOSED TO GO TO CALIFORNIA, WHERE PAPA WAS SURE HE'D FINALLY STRIKE IT RICH . . .

BUT MAMA SENT ME TO STAY WITH UNCLE JERRY INSTEAD.

UNCLE JERRY AND I USED TO HAVE FUN TOGETHER WHEN I WAS LITTLE, BUT I HADN'T SEEN HIM IN YEARS.

I DIDN'T EVEN KNOW IF HE WOULD RECOGNIZE ME.

BUT I SHOULDN'T HAVE WORRIED.

IT'S ABOUT TIME, CHET.

FROM THAT FIRST DAY, UNCLE JERRY HAS MADE ME FEEL RIGHT AT HOME.

BUT I'M *NOT* HOME. I MISS MAMA AND PAPA.

AND IT DOESN'T MATTER HOW MUCH I LOVE UNCLE JERRY OR HOW MANY PEOPLE SHOUT, "SEE YA, CHET!" WHEN THEY LEAVE THE DINER . . .

SOON ENOUGH I'LL HAVE TO GO TO CALIFORNIA.

WILL I EVER REALLY BELONG ANYWHERE?

OR WILL I ALWAYS BE ON MY OWN?

A TINY SPECK IN THE MIDDLE OF THE OCEAN?

31

BEFORE I LEAVE THE DINER ON THURSDAY, UNCLE JERRY DRAWS ME A MAP TO THE CREEK.

I ALMOST THINK I AM LOST . . .

UNTIL I HEAR THE SPLASHING JUST PAST THE TALL GRASS.

THE GUYS WERE RIGHT: THE CREEK'S NOT MUCH. MAYBE TWENTY FEET ACROSS.

I CAN'T EVEN TELL IF IT'S DEEP ENOUGH TO DIVE.

JUMP!

HURRY UP! THE WATER'S PERFECT.

BUT RIGHT AT THIS MOMENT . . .

KER-PLOSH!

CHET! CATCH!

. . . THERE'S NO PLACE ON EARTH I'D RATHER BE.

The next day, after breakfast rush...

WHAT'S WRONG, KIDDO?

WHEN YOUR BUDDIES CAME BY THIS MORNING, IT LOOKED LIKE YOU WERE AVOIDING THEM.

THEY'RE NOT MY BUDDIES.

BECAUSE OF THAT STUNT AT THE CREEK?

YOU HEARD ABOUT THAT?

IT WAS JUST A PRANK. YOU SHOULD BE FLATTERED.

IT MEANS THEY LIKE YOU, THAT YOU'RE ONE OF THEM.

NOW THEY'RE EXPECTING YOU TO GET THEM BACK.

DON'T YOU KNOW HOW THIS WORKS?

NO.

HOW COULD I KNOW?

I'VE NEVER HAD ANY REAL FRIENDS BEFORE.

43

MR. COLTON AND DR. JAY ARE UNCLE JERRY'S OLDEST FRIENDS.

YOU SEEN THE MORNING PAPER?

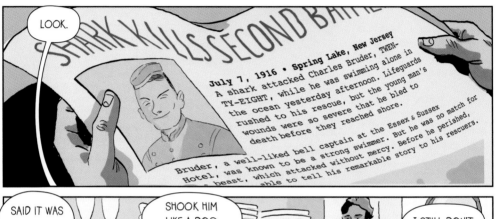

LOOK.

SHARK KILLS SECOND BATHER

July 7, 1916 • Spring Lake, New Jersey

A shark attacked Charles Bruder, TWEN-TY-EIGHT, while he was swimming alone in the ocean yesterday afternoon. Lifeguards rushed to his rescue, but the young man's wounds were so severe that he bled to death before they reached shore.

Bruder, a well-liked bell captain at the Essex & Sussex Hotel, was known to be a strong swimmer. But he was no match for beast, which attacked without mercy. Before he perished, able to tell his remarkable story to his rescuers.

SAID IT WAS A BIG GRAY FELLOW . . .

SNIPPED HIS LEGS CLEAN OFF!

SHOOK HIM LIKE A DOG SHAKES A RAT!

I STILL DON'T BELIEVE IT.

SOMEONE IS COOKING UP THESE STORIES TO SELL NEWSPAPERS.

COULD BE.

BUT MY WIFE'S COUSIN LIVES OUT THERE AND SHE SAYS NOBODY WILL GO NEAR THE OCEAN.

THEY HAVE FISHERMEN WITH RIFLES SHOOTING ANYTHING THAT MOVES.

YOU KNOW WHAT THIS REMINDS ME OF?

THE CREEK DEVIL.

WHAT'S THAT?

OLD-TIMERS SAY THERE'S A MONSTER THAT LIVES DOWN NEAR THE CREEK.

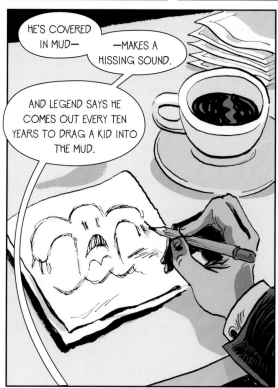

HE'S COVERED IN MUD—

—MAKES A HISSING SOUND.

AND LEGEND SAYS HE COMES OUT EVERY TEN YEARS TO DRAG A KID INTO THE MUD.

PEOPLE BELIEVE THAT?

EVERYONE IN TOWN KNOWS THE LEGEND.

BUT NOBODY REALLY BELIEVES IT.

EXCEPT FOR JERRY HERE.

WHEN WE WERE LITTLE, HE WOULDN'T GO NEAR THAT CREEK!

BAH. I DON'T KNOW WHAT YOU'RE TALKING ABOUT.

DOESN'T SOMEONE NEED A WART REMOVED OR SOMETHING?

IMAGINE . . .

UNCLE JERRY BEING AFRAID OF A MADE-UP MONSTER!

SUDDENLY, I GET AN IDEA . . .

FOR THE GREATEST PRANK EVER.

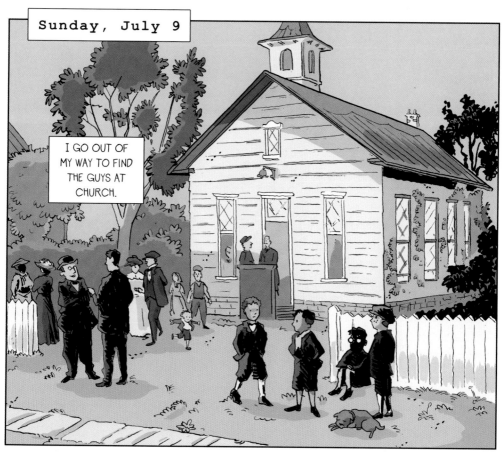

Sunday, July 9

I GO OUT OF MY WAY TO FIND THE GUYS AT CHURCH.

WE DIDN'T MEAN TO SCARE YOU SO BAD.

WE ALWAYS DO PRANKS!

IT WAS ALL IN GOOD FUN.

48

I WAVE TO MINNIE MARSTON.

BUT THERE'S NO TIME FOR GIRLS.

THIS MORNING, I PACKED MY BAG WITH A BOTTLE OF KETCHUP . . .

A HAT FROM THE DINER . . .

AND ONE OF MY OLD WORK BOOTS.

EVERYTHING I NEED.

SO FAR, SO GOOD.

I LOOK FOR THE SLIMIEST MUD I CAN FIND.

THEN I HEAR THE GUYS.

57

I SIT ON UNCLE JERRY'S PORCH A LONG TIME.

I WONDER WHAT MAMA AND PAPA ARE DOING.

THERE YOU ARE!

SO THERE WAS SOME EXCITEMENT AT THE CREEK, I HEAR.

POOR DEWEY CAME RUNNING DOWN MAIN STREET WHITE AS A GHOST.

SCREAMING ABOUT THE CREEK DEVIL. HIS MAMA CALLED DR. JAY.

UNCLE JERRY PROBABLY ALREADY SENT A TELEGRAM TO MAMA AND PAPA . . .

PLANNING TO SHIP ME DIRECTLY TO CALIFORNIA.

I SUPPOSE I SHOULD START PACKING.

I WENT TOO FAR.

I GUESS YOU DID.

HEH-HEH-HEH-HEH . . .

SORRY . . .

BUT THAT LOOK ON DEWEY'S FACE . . .

IT WAS A GOOD PRANK.

MAYBE A LITTLE TOO GRUESOME.

BUT DARN GOOD.

HEH-HEH . . .

SOB

IT'S ALL RIGHT . . .

NO. I NEED TO LEAVE.

I DON'T BELONG HERE.

OF COURSE YOU DO!

WHY DO YOU THINK I BEGGED YOUR MAMA TO LET YOU COME STAY WITH ME?

66

"I KNOW YOU WILL."

FOR TWO DAYS, I WAIT FOR THE GUYS TO COME IN . . .

SLAM!

BUT THEY NEVER EVEN WALK BY.

ON THE THIRD DAY, UNCLE JERRY CLOSES THE DINER EARLY.

HOTTEST DAY THIS SUMMER! THE ICE IS MELTED, THE MILK'S CURDLED, AND YOU COULD COOK A FLAPJACK ON THE FLOOR.

I'M GOING HOME TO STICK MY HEAD UNDER THE WATER PUMP.

CLOSED

ELM HIL

I HEAD FOR THE CREEK, SURE I'LL FIND THE GUYS PLAYING BALL IN THE WATER . . .

BUT THE SWIMMING HOLE IS QUIET.

THEN I REMEMBER THE TIME. THEY'RE STILL AT WORK AT THE TILE FACTORY.

THEIR SHIFT WON'T BE OVER FOR ANOTHER HOUR.

THE SPLOTCHES OF KETCHUP ON THE DOCK ARE STILL THERE.

THEY LOOK EVEN MORE LIKE BLOOD NOW.

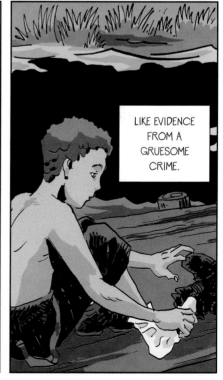

LIKE EVIDENCE FROM A GRUESOME CRIME.

I'D BETTER CLEAN IT UP . . .

SPLASH!

ERASE ALL REMINDERS OF THE PRANK BEFORE THE GUYS GET HERE.

SCRATCH
SCRATCH

BY THE TIME I'M DONE, I NEED A SWIM TO COOL OFF.

IT'S PEACEFUL WITHOUT ALL THE SPLASHING AND SHOUTING.

I THINK ABOUT THE DAY PAPA TAUGHT ME TO SWIM IN THE MISSISSIPPI.

MAMA WAVED AND CLAPPED FROM THE RIVERBANK.

BUT JUST AS I START BACK FOR THE DOCK . . .

THEN I SEE IT.

A FIN.

I'VE GOT TO BE SEEING THINGS.

IS THIS ANOTHER PRANK?

SID, SNEAKING UP ON ME AGAIN?

NO.

THAT'S NO TILE.

ITS JAWS SNAP OPEN AND CLOSED.

SNAP SNAP S

IT THRASHES, LIKE IT'S TRYING TO PUSH ITSELF UP ONTO THE BANK.

I WANT TO GET UP AND RUN . . .

BUT I'M FROZEN TO THE GROUND.

SPLASH

SNAP

THWACK

IT HOVERS FOR A
SECOND ON THE
SURFACE . . .

THEN IT DISAPPEARS.

I DON'T EVEN
BOTHER TO LACE
MY BOOTS.

BLOOD
POUNDING IN
MY EARS . . .

I RUN.

SOMEHOW, I FIND MY WAY
TO MAIN STREET . . .

IT'S THE HEAT, MY BOY. IT'S DRIVING US ALL A LITTLE MAD.

TAKE A DRINK, SON—

NO!

WE HAVE TO WARN PEOPLE!

CHET...

THERE'S SO MUCH GARBAGE FLOATING IN THAT CREEK.

IT COULD HAVE BEEN A PLANK FROM THE DOCK, OR A BARREL, OR—

NO! IT WAS A SHARK!

I THINK MAYBE ALL THOSE PRANKS ARE GETTING TO YOU.

I KNOW I MUST SOUND CRAZY.

NOBODY WILL BELIEVE ME.

WHY WOULD THEY?

IT'S IMPOSSIBLE.

I'VE WASTED ENOUGH TIME ALREADY.

YES?

WHAT IS THIS ABOUT?

S-SORRY, SIR.

I DIDN'T MEAN TO BOTHER YOU.

HE'S LOOKING AT ME LIKE HE'S NEVER SEEN ME BEFORE.

"MIND LIKE SWISS CHEESE," UNCLE JERRY SAID . . .

BUT I HAVE TO TRY.

CAPTAIN . . .

I SAW A SHARK. IN THE CREEK.

IT CRASHED INTO ME.

DOES HE EVEN KNOW WHERE HE IS?

I KNOW IT SOUNDS IMPOSSIBLE, SIR.

IT DOESN'T MAKE ANY SENSE AT ALL.

SURE IT DOES.

THE CREEK EMPTIES OUT INTO RARITAN BAY, WHICH LEADS RIGHT TO THE ATLANTIC.

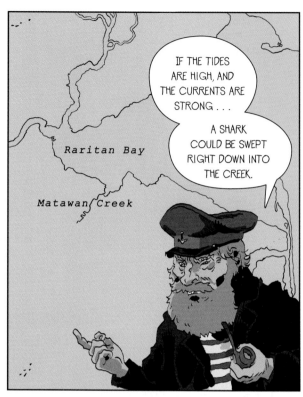

Raritan Bay

Matawan Creek

IF THE TIDES ARE HIGH, AND THE CURRENTS ARE STRONG . . .

A SHARK COULD BE SWEPT RIGHT DOWN INTO THE CREEK.

I SAW IT, CAPTAIN.

IT WAS HUGE, AND ITS EYES, JUST LIKE YOU SAID—

KILLER EYES.

YES.

WHY ARE YOU STANDING HERE, SON?

WE NEED TO WARN PEOPLE!

THAT SHARK IS STILL OUT THERE.

IF I'D BEEN A STEP SLOWER IN THE WATER, I'D BE DEAD—

—JUST ANOTHER NAME IN THE NEWSPAPER.

GET OUT! GET OUT NOW!

108

THEN I NOTICE SID.

GET OUT!

HURRY!

COME ON! *IT'S COMING!*

BUT SID SEEMS STUCK . . .

COME *ON!*

HYPNOTIZED.

114

BLACK EYES ALMOST GLOWING.

WHiRRRRRRRRR

I HEAR A MOTOR IN THE DISTANCE.

AFTER AN
ETERNITY—

—I FINALLY
COME FREE.

BUT I HAVE TO GET
ONE MORE LOOK.

PEOPLE SEEM TO MOVE IN SLOW MOTION.

I HEAR VOICES . . .

AND A MOTORBOAT . . .

BUT SUDDENLY I'M SO, SO TIRED.

THE GUYS KEEP SAYING MY NAME OVER AND OVER.

CHET!

CHET!

CHET!

EVERYTHING LOOKS FOGGY . . .

WHAT AM I DOING IN A PILE OF KETCHUP?

DIDN'T I CLEAN THAT UP?

WHY IS THE PUDDLE GETTING BIGGER?

BUT IT ISN'T KETCHUP.

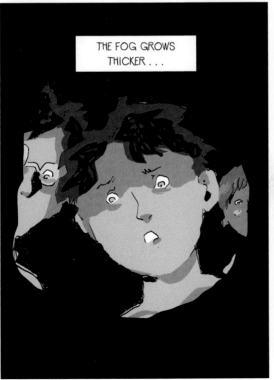

THE FOG GROWS THICKER . . .

The Matawan Journal

JULY 13, 1916

SHARK KILLS TWO IN NEW JERSEY CREEK

A THIRD BOY SURVIVES, BUT INJURIES ARE GRAVE

Lester Stillwell

Mr. Stanley Fisher

Elm Hills, New Jersey

A boy and a young man were killed yesterday, July 12, by a monster shark that made a shocking appearance in the Matawan Creek in New Jersey. **Lester Stillwell**, 11, was killed while swimming with friends in the town of Matawan. Minutes later, **Stanley Fisher**, 24, was killed as he bravely attempted to rescue young Lester.

Farther up the creek, **Chet Roscow**, 10, encountered the shark as he swam by himself. He managed to escape and ran into town to alert residents. His cries of warning were ignored, with most residents dismissing his story as a prank. The boy did not give up and later attempted to warn his friends, who were swimming behind the Templer Tile Factory. It was during these efforts that the lad fell into the jaws of the monstrous shark.

He was rescued moments later when Captain Thomas A. Wilson shot at the shark with a Civil War musket, scaring the beast away.

The brave youth was rushed to Saint Peter's Hospital in New Brunswick. Injuries to his leg are described as extremely grave.

AM I ASLEEP?

AM I AWAKE?

AM I ALIVE OR DEAD?

PICTURES FLOAT IN AND OUT OF MY MIND . . .

WHITE WALLS . . .

WHITE SHEETS . . .

DOCTORS . . .

A NURSE WITH A SOFT VOICE.

AND UNCLE JERRY, ALWAYS BY MY SIDE.

DAYS PASS BEFORE I UNDERSTAND WHAT HAPPENED.

SAINT PETER'S HOSPITAL

THE SHARK RIPPED AWAY PART OF MY CALF.

ANOTHER FEW SECONDS AND IT WOULD HAVE TAKEN OFF MY WHOLE LEG.

IT WILL HEAL.

IT WILL TAKE SOME TIME, BUT YOUR LEG WILL HEAL.

"THE MIRACLE KID."

THAT'S WHAT THE NEWSPAPERS ARE CALLING YOU.

DOESN'T FEEL LIKE A MIRACLE WHEN IT HURTS SO MUCH . . .

IT'S TRUE!

THE BOY WHO WAS ATTACKED A MILE DOWN THE CREEK AND THE MAN WHO JUMPED IN TO SAVE HIM—

THEY WEREN'T AS LUCKY AS YOU WERE, CHET.

MY LEG HURTS WORSE THAN WHEN THE SHARK WAS BITING ME.

AND THE PAIN MEDICINE MAKES ME FEEL SICK.

I WISH MAMA AND PAPA WERE HERE.

THEY TOOK THE FIRST TRAIN AS SOON AS THEY HEARD.

THEY'LL BE HERE BEFORE YOU KNOW IT.

THE DOCTOR SAYS I'LL HAVE A LIMP.

THAT'S RIGHT—JUST LIKE MINE.

BUT I KNOW IT WON'T SLOW YOU DOWN A BIT.

SLEEP WELL, KIDDO.

I LIE THERE . . .

BUT I DON'T WANT TO SLEEP.

EVERY TIME I FALL ASLEEP, I WAKE UP SHAKING.

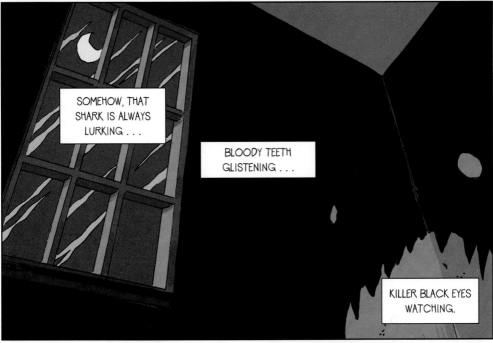

SOMEHOW, THAT SHARK IS ALWAYS LURKING . . .

BLOODY TEETH GLISTENING . . .

KILLER BLACK EYES WATCHING.

EVEN THOUGH MY ROOM IS FILLED WITH FLOWERS AND CARDS FROM ALL OVER THE WORLD—

—I'VE NEVER FELT SO ALONE.

CHET!

HEY, MAKE ROOM ON THAT BED!

IT'S NOT THE SAME AT HOME WITHOUT YOU.

I'LL BE IN THE HALLWAY, KIDDO.

I THINK THAT PRETTY NURSE LIKES ME.

THEY DYNAMITED THE CREEK!

A GUY CAUGHT A SHARK IN THE BAY, SAYS IT'S THE SAME SHARK!

"IT WAS TEN FEET LONG!"

"THEY CUT OPEN ITS STOMACH."

"THEY FOUND HUMAN BONES!"

CAPTAIN WILSON IS A CELEBRITY.

REPORTERS ARE COMING FROM ALL OVER THE WORLD TO TALK TO HIM!

I'VE ALREADY HEARD A LOT OF THIS FROM UNCLE JERRY . . .

BUT I HOPE THEY NEVER STOP TALKING.

YOU KNOW . . .

I HAD AN IDEA, THOUGHT I'D MENTION IT TO YOU.

MAYBE YOUR PAPA WOULD LIKE TO HELP ME RUN THE DINER.

IT'S A BUSY PLACE. I THINK HE MIGHT ENJOY IT.

WE DO WELL ENOUGH, AND I SURE WOULDN'T MIND HAVING MORE TIME TO MYSELF.

YOU MEAN . . . ?

YOUR PAPA MIGHT DECIDE IT'S TIME TO SETTLE DOWN.

I'M NOT SURE HE'LL SAY YES, BUT IT'S WORTH A TRY.

DON'T YOU THINK?

I OPEN MY MOUTH TO SAY SOMETHING—

BUT THE WORDS JUST STICK TOGETHER.

SO I NOD.

OKAY, THEN, KIDDO.

IT'S A PLAN.

TIME TO GET YOU BOYS HOME TO YOUR MAMAS.

SEE YOU TOMORROW, CHET.

I LIE THERE FOR A LONG TIME.

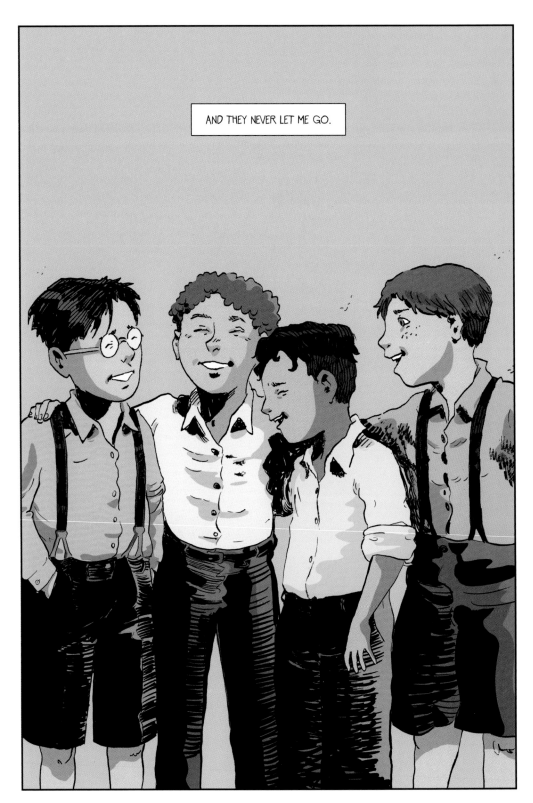

TURN THE PAGE
TO READ MORE ABOUT
SHARKS AND THE DEADLY

SHARK ATTACKS
OF 1916

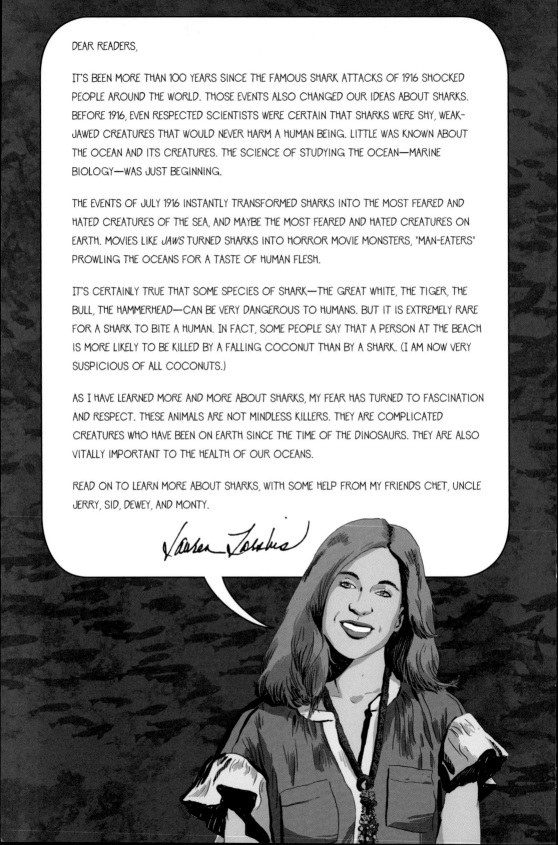

THE REAL-LIFE SHARK ATTACKS OF 1916

THE NEW JERSEY ATTACKS BEGAN AMERICA'S FASCINATION WITH SHARKS. HERE'S A TIMELINE OF THE REAL-LIFE CHARACTERS AND EVENTS OF THAT TERRIFYING SUMMER.

Matawan●
July 12

Spring Lake●
July 6

Beach Haven●
July 1

Atlantic Ocean

SHARK ATTACKS ON THE JERSEY SHORE, 1916

JULY 1:
CHARLES E. VANSANT, A 25-YEAR-OLD BUSINESSMAN, IS ATTACKED WHILE VACATIONING IN BEACH HAVEN WITH HIS FATHER AND SISTERS. A LIFEGUARD TRIES TO SAVE HIM, BUT MR. VANSANT DOES NOT SURVIVE.

THE ESSEX & SUSSEX HOTEL, SPRING LAKE, NJ

JULY 6: FIVE DAYS LATER, ABOUT 50 MILES UP THE COAST IN ANOTHER POPULAR VACATION TOWN CALLED SPRING LAKE, 28-YEAR-OLD **CHARLES BRUDER** GOES FOR A SWIM ON HIS LUNCH BREAK. A SHARK ATTACKS HIM 130 YARDS FROM SHORE. LIFEGUARDS TRY TO SAVE HIM BUT HE DIES IN THE BOAT ON THE WAY BACK TO THE BEACH.

MR. BRUDER WORKED AT A FANCY HOTEL BY THE BEACH.

CHARLES E. VANSANT
AUGUST 22, 1892–JULY 1, 1916

JULY 8: A SHARK IS SPOTTED A FEW MILES NORTH, IN ASBURY PARK. A LIFEGUARD GETS IN A BOAT AND BEATS THE SHARK WITH AN OAR TO SCARE IT AWAY.

THE MATAWAN ATTACKS

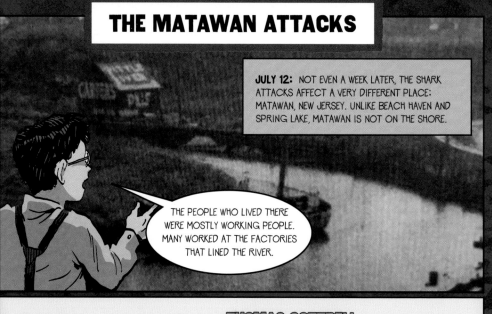

JULY 12: NOT EVEN A WEEK LATER, THE SHARK ATTACKS AFFECT A VERY DIFFERENT PLACE: MATAWAN, NEW JERSEY. UNLIKE BEACH HAVEN AND SPRING LAKE, MATAWAN IS NOT ON THE SHORE.

THE PEOPLE WHO LIVED THERE WERE MOSTLY WORKING PEOPLE. MANY WORKED AT THE FACTORIES THAT LINED THE RIVER.

ABOUT 1:30 P.M.: A RETIRED SEA CAPTAIN NAMED **THOMAS COTTRELL** SPOTS A SHARK WHILE CROSSING A BRIDGE OVER MATAWAN CREEK. HE RUNS INTO TOWN TO WARN OTHERS, BUT NO ONE BELIEVES HIM. THE IDEA THAT A SHARK COULD BE IN THE CREEK SEEMS IMPOSSIBLE.

ABOUT 2 P.M.: HAVING LEFT EARLY FROM HIS JOB AT THE BASKET FACTORY, ELEVEN-YEAR-OLD **LESTER STILLWELL** IS SWIMMING IN THE CREEK WITH SOME FRIENDS WHEN A SHARK PULLS HIM UNDER. HIS FRIENDS RUSH UP MAIN STREET. A SHOP OWNER NAMED **STANLEY FISHER** DOUBTS THERE IS A SHARK, BUT FEARS LESTER IS DROWNING. HE GRABS TWO OTHER MEN AND THEY DASH TO THE CREEK. A CROWD FOLLOWS.

ABOUT 2:30 P.M.: HALF A MILE DOWN THE CREEK, FOURTEEN-YEAR-OLD **JOSEPH DUNN** IS SWIMMING WITH HIS BROTHER AND SOME FRIENDS WHEN THEY HEAR SHOUTING ABOUT A SHARK. THE BOYS RUSH TO GET OUT OF THE WATER, BUT THE SHARK GRABS JOSEPH'S LOWER LEFT LEG. BYSTANDERS PULL JOSEPH TO SAFETY AND RUSH HIM TO THE HOSPITAL. HE SPENDS TWO MONTHS RECOVERING, BUT SURVIVES.

LESTER STILLWELL
JULY 19, 1904–JULY 12, 1916

JUST LIKE ME!

JOSEPH DUNN
MARCH 19, 1902– APRIL 1, 1982

BACK AT THE SITE OF LESTER'S DISAPPEARANCE, MORE THAN 30 MINUTES HAVE PASSED AND MR. FISHER KNOWS LESTER CANNOT HAVE SURVIVED. STILL, HE WANTS TO RECOVER LESTER'S BODY FOR HIS FAMILY. A SHARK ATTACKS HIM WHILE HE SEARCHES.

FOR THIS REASON—DIVING TO FIND LESTER EVEN WHEN HE KNEW HE WASN'T ALIVE—MANY PEOPLE CONSIDERED MR. FISHER A HERO.

MR. FISHER IS BADLY INJURED AND NEEDS SURGERY AT THE BIG HOSPITAL SEVERAL TOWNS AWAY. BUT THE NEXT TRAIN IS NOT FOR TWO HOURS.

STANLEY FISHER
APRIL 12, 1892–JULY 12, 1916

6:45 P.M.: THOUGH SURGEONS TRY TO SAVE MR. FISHER'S LIFE, HE DIES FROM BLOOD LOSS AND SHOCK.

JULY 13: MEMBERS OF THE MATAWAN COMMUNITY BLAST **DYNAMITE UNDERWATER** IN AN ATTEMPT TO KILL THE SHARK.

JULY 14: A MAN CATCHES A 7.5-FOOT, 325-POUND YOUNG GREAT WHITE SHARK IN RARITAN BAY, A FEW MILES FROM THE MOUTH OF MATAWAN CREEK. IT HAS HUMAN REMAINS IN ITS STOMACH. SCIENTISTS DUB IT THE **"JERSEY MAN-EATER."**

DID YOU KNOW?

MANY PEOPLE BELIEVE THAT THE BESTSELLING BOOK—AND EVENTUALLY CLASSIC HIT-MOVIE—JAWS WAS INSPIRED BY THE 1916 ATTACKS. BUT THE AUTHOR, PETER BENCHLEY, DENIES THIS.

MR. BENCHLEY HAS EVEN DEVOTED HIS LIFE TO PROTECTING SHARKS!

MORE SHARK ATTACK FACTS

A TIGER SHARK

A HAMMERHEAD SHARK

OF THE MORE THAN 350 KNOWN SPECIES OF SHARKS, **ONLY FOUR SPECIES** ARE PARTICULARLY PRONE TO ATTACK A HUMAN: THE BULL SHARK, THE GREAT WHITE, THE TIGER SHARK, AND THE HAMMERHEAD.

SHARK ATTACKS ARE VERY RARE! EACH YEAR, **ONLY ABOUT FIVE PEOPLE** DIE IN ENCOUNTERS WITH SHARKS.

IN CONTRAST, ABOUT 125,000 PEOPLE DIE OF SNAKEBITES EACH YEAR.

FLORIDA IS THE NUMBER-ONE SHARK ATTACK STATE IN THE U.S., WITH AN AVERAGE OF THIRTY ATTACKS A YEAR. CALIFORNIA, HAWAII, NORTH CAROLINA, AND SOUTH CAROLINA HAVE ALL HAD A FEW ATTACKS TOO.

THERE HAS NOT BEEN ANOTHER FATAL ATTACK RECORDED IN NEW JERSEY SINCE 1926.

SOME SCIENTISTS BELIEVE THAT MOST SHARKS **DON'T MEAN TO ATTACK HUMANS** BUT MISTAKE SURFERS OR SWIMMERS FOR LARGE SEA MAMMALS, LIKE SEALS.

THIS COULD EXPLAIN WHY MOST SHARK ATTACKS ON HUMANS **ARE NOT FATAL**—A SHARK TAKES ONE BITE, REALIZES ITS MISTAKE, AND SWIMS AWAY.

SHARK SAFETY

> IT'S USUALLY SAFE TO SWIM IN THE OCEAN, BUT IF YOU ARE IN SHARK TERRITORY, FOLLOW THESE TIPS TO STAY SAFE.

SWIM ONLY ON BEACHES WHERE THERE IS A LIFEGUARD. AND IF SHARKS HAVE BEEN SEEN IN THE AREA, STAY OUT OF THE WATER.

SWIM IN GROUPS. MOST SHARK ATTACKS HAPPEN TO PEOPLE SWIMMING ALONE IN THE OCEAN.

IF YOU ARE BLEEDING, STAY OUT OF THE WATER. SHARKS CAN DETECT ONE DROP OF BLOOD IN AN OLYMPIC-SIZE POOL.

LEAVE YOUR JEWELRY ON LAND. FLASHING METAL CAN ALSO ATTRACT SHARKS.

AVOID SWIMMING AT NIGHT OR AT DUSK. THIS IS WHEN SHARKS FEED.

WHO IS MORE DANGEROUS?

EVERY YEAR **HUMANS KILL NEARLY 100 MILLION SHARKS,** MAINLY FOR THEIR FINS, WHICH ARE A PRIZED INGREDIENT IN SHARK FIN SOUP. MANY SHARK SPECIES ARE IN DANGER OF DISAPPEARING FROM OUR OCEANS FOREVER.

SHARKS ARE IMPORTANT TO THE **HEALTH OF OUR OCEANS.** IF BIG SHARKS DISAPPEAR, THE BALANCE OF LIFE IN OUR OCEANS WILL BE DAMAGED. RATHER THAN FEAR SHARKS, HUMANS NEED TO WORK TO PROTECT THEM FROM OVERFISHING AND OCEAN POLLUTION.

A GREAT WHITE SHARK

> SHARKS CAN BE DANGEROUS, BUT THEY NEED OUR PROTECTION!

SELECTED BIBLIOGRAPHY

Capuzzo, Michael, *Close to Shore: The Terrifying Shark Attacks of 1916*, New York: Crown Books, 2003.

Fernicola, Richard G., and Guilford, M. D., *Twelve Days of Terror: A Definitive Investigation of the 1916 New Jersey Shark Attacks*, Connecticut: The Lyons Press, 2001.

Peschak, Thomas, *Sharks and People: Exploring Our Relationship with the Most Feared Fish in the Sea*, Chicago: The University of Chicago Press, 2013.

Savolaine, John Allan, *Stanley Fisher: Shark Attack Hero of a Bygone Age: How Brave Men Faced a Relentless Killer Shark in a Small New Jersey Town the Summer of 1916*, Middletown, NJ: Riverside Prints, 2016.

Gambion, Megan, "The Shark Attacks That Were the Inspiration for Jaws," *Smithsonian*, 2012.

Wilkinson, Alec, "Cape Fear," *The New Yorker*, September 9, 2013.

MORE SHARK BOOKS YOU MIGHT LIKE

Capuzzo, Michael, *Close to Shore: The Terrifying Shark Attacks of 1916*, New York: Crown Books, 2003.

Tarshis, Lauren, *I Survived the Shark Attacks of 1916*, New York: Scholastic, 2010.

Tarshis, Lauren, *I Survived True Stories: Nature Attacks!*, New York: Scholastic, 2015.

OTHER I SURVIVED GRAPHIC NOVELS

Tarshis, Lauren, *I Survived the Sinking of the Titanic, 1912: The Graphic Novel*, New York: Scholastic, 2020.

FEATURING ME, GEORGE!

AND ME, PHOEBE!

LAUREN TARSHIS'S

NEW YORK TIMES BESTSELLING I SURVIVED SERIES TELLS STORIES OF YOUNG PEOPLE AND THEIR RESILIENCE AND STRENGTH IN THE MIDST OF UNIMAGINABLE DISASTERS AND TIMES OF TURMOIL. LAUREN HAS BROUGHT HER SIGNATURE WARMTH, INTEGRITY, AND EXHAUSTIVE RESEARCH TO TOPICS SUCH AS THE BATTLE OF D-DAY, THE AMERICAN REVOLUTION, HURRICANE KATRINA, THE BOMBING OF PEARL HARBOR, AND OTHER WORLD EVENTS. LAUREN LIVES IN CONNECTICUT WITH HER FAMILY, AND CAN BE FOUND ONLINE AT LAURENTARSHIS.COM.

GEORGIA BALL

HAS WRITTEN COMICS FOR MANY OF HER FAVORITE CHILDHOOD CHARACTERS, INCLUDING STRAWBERRY SHORTCAKE, TRANSFORMERS, LITTLEST PET SHOP, MY LITTLE PONY, AND THE DISNEY PRINCESSES. IN ADDITION TO ADAPTING LAUREN TARSHIS'S I SURVIVED SERIES TO GRAPHIC NOVELS, GEORGIA WRITES ABOUT HISTORICAL EVENTS SUCH AS THE WORLD WAR II BATTLES OF KURSK AND GUADALCANAL. GEORGIA LIVES WITH HER HUSBAND, DAUGHTER, AND RAMBUNCTIOUS PETS IN NORTHERN WASHINGTON STATE. VISIT HER ONLINE AT GEORGIABALLAUTHOR.COM.

HAUS STUDIO

WAS FOUNDED IN 1997 BY A GROUP OF FRIENDS WHO SELF-PUBLISHED THEIR OWN COMICS. THEY ARE LOCATED IN BUENOS AIRES, ARGENTINA, BUT COLLABORATE WITH WRITERS AND PUBLISHERS AROUND THE WORLD. IN ADDITION TO THEIR ILLUSTRATION WORK, THE TEAM RUNS AN ART SCHOOL AND HAS ORGANIZED COMIC BOOK CONVENTIONS AND OTHER EXHIBITIONS IN LATIN AMERICA. HAUS STUDIO ARTISTS CONSIDER THEMSELVES STORYTELLERS MORE THAN ARTISTS, AND THEREFORE LOVE WORKING ON PROJECTS WITH RICH STORIES TO TELL.

DISCOVER THE SERIES THAT STARTED IT ALL!

I SURVIVED

WHEN DISASTER STRIKES, HEROES ARE MADE!

I SURVIVED
TRUE STORIES

REAL KIDS. REAL DISASTERS.